To Freya

From...Mummy...

It was Christmas Eve and Freya
was snug and warm in her cosy bed.
She was trying so hard to go to sleep,
but she could hear strange noises.

It wasn't the sound of sleigh bells.
It wasn't the sound of reindeer hoofs on the roof.
t wasn't even the sound of Santa unpacking his sack.

It was more of a

HARRUMPH!

and an

OOF!

It was no use.

There would be no sleep for Freya
until she had found out what
was making that noise.

Freya crept down the stairs
and peered into the living room.
There were three stockings
hanging from the fireplace.

One of them belonged
to Freya. But where had
the other two come from?
Suddenly, a muffled voice
came from the chimney.

Freya

"Oh, dear.
I'm even
more
stuck now!"

There was a scuffling sound
from behind the Christmas
tree, and Freya jumped
when a small elf appeared.

Freya

"Uh, hello," said the elf. "I guess you've caught us!"

Freya listened as the elf explained
that Santa was stuck in the chimney.
The elf had tried to pull him out, but the
only things that had come down so far
were Santa's boots and trousers!

"I can help you," suggested Freya.
"I'll hold Santa's feet and we can both pull."
The elf agreed. "Between us we might
be able to get him unstuck."

Freya firmly grasped both of Santa's feet.
Suddenly a light went on upstairs.
"Freya, is that you?" called her mum.
"Back to bed now, please, or Santa won't come!"

At that moment
Santa shot back up
the chimney… with
Freya still hanging
onto his feet!

The poor elf could not believe his eyes.
But there was no time to think...
Freya's mum was coming
out of her bedroom.

"I'm coming!" squeaked the elf. He hurried
up the stairs and jumped into Freya's bed,
pulling the covers over his head.
"Night night, sweetie," said Freya's mum.

Meanwhile, up on the roof, Santa and Freya had landed in a heap. The clever reindeer had hooked their reins under Santa's arms and pulled as hard as they could.

"Good work!" said Santa, brushing himself off. "No more mince pies for me tonight!"

Freya scrambled to her feet, but Santa was so busy that he didn't notice Freya and the elf had switched places!

"I think we had better deliver the rest of the presents first," said Santa, "and leave this house for last."

Santa climbed into the driver's seat.

"Elf, you get the presents ready for our next destination," he called over his shoulder. "But I'm not Elf..." replied Freya.

Santa wasn't listening.
He was talking to the reindeer.
"Up, up and away!" Santa called,
and the reindeer took off before
Freya had time to explain.

Freya held on tight as the
sleigh soared high over the rooftops
and into the night sky.

Surrounded by sacks, Freya was
so busy working out which presents were
which that there was no time to let Santa
know a mistake had been made.

There were **big**
presents for the cities,

and **SHINY** presents
for the towns.

There were **ODD**-shaped
presents for the villages,

and **unusual**
presents for the farms.

To
Freya

As they landed at their next stop, Santa decided that he couldn't risk getting stuck in a chimney again.

"Elf, I think you had better make the deliveries from now on," Santa said. "I'll sort the presents."

Freya *shimmied* down chimneys.

She **squeezed** through cat flaps.

And, if all else failed, she used Santa's *magic* key to let herself in.

In each house Freya picked up the mince pies to take to Mrs Claus and carrots for the reindeer.

Finally there was just one sack left, and
Santa still hadn't realised his mistake!
The sleigh headed back over the
rooftops to Freya's house.

Sliding down her chimney with
a sack of her own presents was
the most fun Freya had ever had.

She put her presents under
the Christmas tree, then picked
up Santa's trousers and boots
and placed them in the sack.

Freya

"Psst! Elf, where are you?" whispered Freya.

A very happy Elf appeared, rubbing his eyes.
"I've had such a nice nap," he said.
Freya handed over the sack and
waved as Elf disappeared
up the chimney.

Back in her cosy bed, Freya could
hear the sounds of jingling sleigh bells,
reindeer hoofs on the roof and, very faintly,

"Ho, ho, ho!

Merry Christmas!"

Or was that,

"Ho, ho, ho!
Yummy mince pies!"?

Write your name on the labels.

To Freya

To Freya

TO Freya

To Freya

To Freya

To Freya

To Freya

To Freya

To Freya

Draw yourself as an elf.

ME FREYA
THE ELF

AGE 7

31.12.18

2018

December

Written by Katherine Sully
Illustrated by Julia Seal
Designed by Nicola Moore

This edition published by HOMETOWN WORLD in 2018
Hometown World Ltd
1 Queen Street
Bath
BA1 1HE

www.hometownworld.co.uk

Follow us @hometownworldbooks

ISBN 978-1-78553-605-2
Printed in Italy
HTW_PO201814

put **me**
in the **story**®
Bestselling books starring your child!
www.putmeinthestory.co.uk